HOPSCOTCH HISTORIES

Toby and the
Great Fire
of London

First published in 2007 by
Franklin Watts
338 Euston Road
London
NW1 3BH

Franklin Watts Australia
Level 17/207 Kent Street
Sydney
NSW 2000

A CIP catalogue record for this book is available
from the British Library.

ISBN 978 0 7496 7079 5 (hbk)
ISBN 978 0 7496 7410 6 (pbk)

Series Editor: Melanie Palmer
Series Advisor: Dr Barrie Wade
Series Designer: Peter Scoulding

Printed in China

Franklin Watts is a division of
Hachette Children's Books.

HOPSCOTCH HISTORIES

Toby and the
Great Fire
of London

by Margaret Nash and Jane Cope

W
FRANKLIN WATTS
LONDON•SYDNEY

About this book

Most of the characters in this book are made up, but the subject is based on real events in history. The Great Fire of London broke out on 2nd September 1666. It burned for three nights and four days and destroyed most of London! The fire started in a baker's shop in Pudding Lane and quickly spread across the city, destroying thousands of homes, churches and London landmarks including St Paul's Cathedral. Luckily most people escaped – only about 5 people died – but thousands were left homeless. Samuel Pepys (1633–1703) saw the events and recorded them in his famous diary.

Toby was asleep after a long day's work. He lived above his master's shop in London.

"Toby! Get up!" shouted Master.
You've left the book for Mr Pepys
here, foolish boy! Take it at once,
it's for his diary!"

"Oh no!" cried Toby.

He leapt out of bed, grabbed the

book and ran out into the street.

The night was hot, but there was a
strong breeze blowing. People were
out in the street. Some were running.

Toby looked up. There were
clouds of smoke and a red sky.
Whatever was the matter?

Toby ran round the corner.

"FIRE! FIRE!" shouted an old lady.

She was still in her night-gown.

"London's burning!" cried a boy.

"And the river's full of boats."

Toby saw the flames. He ran on.

The streets were full of carts and
choked with smoke. Toby pushed
past the crowds of people.
He must find Mr Pepys!

At last, Toby found Mr Pepys's
house and knocked on his door.

But no one came.

"Is anyone in?" called Toby.

No one answered. He climbed the
wall. Up and up he went to the top.

Then he saw a terrible sight:
an arc of flames spreading all
over the city of London.

Toby turned round and saw Mr Pepys putting bottles into a pit! Toby was so surprised, he wobbled and had to jump down from the wall.

He landed by the pit, but the book
landed ... IN the pit!

"OH NO!" cried Toby.

"Hey! This pit is for my wine and cheese," said Mr Pepys. "It's to keep them safe from the fire.

And I don't want my diary
stinking of cheese!" he added.
"PHEW! That cheese really does
pong," said Toby.

Toby jumped down into the pit and got the book out for Mr Pepys.

"Look lad, this fire looks bad!"
said Mr Pepys. "We need to help
stop it spreading. Follow me!"
Off they ran.

By now all the noisy, smoky
streets were very busy.
Toby and Mr Pepys squeezed
past a cow carrying children.

They pushed past bleating goats.

They did not stop until they
reached St Paul's. People were
moving books out to safety.

In the distance, Toby could hear explosions. Houses were being blown up to stop the fire spreading.

A man covered in soot arrived
and climbed down from his
sooty horse.

"Who is this stranger?" said Toby.

"Don't you know?" said Mr Pepys.

"It's King Charles II of England!"

"Take this bucket!" said the King.
"Help me fight this monster of
a fire."

With the King, Mr Pepys, and many other helpers, Toby tried to put out the fire. They all worked day and night until the fire died.

Three days later, Toby returned to
the shop. His master was amazed!
"Oh, thank goodness you're back!
I thought the fire had got you!"

"Not me, Sir. I've been helping

Mr Pepys and the King!" said Toby

"But I do need a good rest."

"And a good wash too!" said Master.

Hopscotch has been specially designed to fit the requirements of the National Literacy Strategy. It offers real books by top authors and illustrators for children developing their reading skills. There are 49 Hopscotch stories to choose from:

* hardback